Princess Florecita and the Iron Shoes

A Spanish Fairy Tale

by John Warren Stewig

illustrated by K. Wendy Popp

Apple Soup Books

AN IMPRINT OF ALFRED A. KNOPF

NEW YORK

To Louise M., who sets out on journeys fearlessly.
—J. W. S.

I dedicate this book to Princess Theresa, my grandmother, and all princesses like her who wore iron boots
to their journey's end so that their granddaughters and great-granddaughters would not have to.

To Princesses Zoë, Nichole, Katie, Lindsay, Robin, and Allison, and Princes Tony, Wendell, and Nicholas,
I wish a safe and loving journey.

—K. W. P.

APPLE SOUP BOOKS IS A TRADEMARK OF ALFRED A. KNOPF, INC.

Text copyright © 1995 by John Warren Stewig
Illustrations copyright © 1995 by K. Wendy Popp

All rights reserved under International and Pan-American Copyright Conventions.
Published in the United States of America by Alfred A. Knopf, Inc., New York,
and simultaneously in Canada by Random House of Canada Limited, Toronto.
Distributed by Random House, Inc., New York.

Library of Congress Cataloging-in-Publication Data
Stewig, John W.
Princess Florecita and the iron shoes / by John Warren Stewig ; illustrated by K. Wendy Popp.
p. cm.
Apple Soup Books
Summary: A princess braves many perils to wake an enchanted sleeping prince.
ISBN 0-679-84775-8 (trade) — ISBN 0-679-94775-2 (lib. bdg.)
[1. Fairy tales.]
I. Popp, K. Wendy, ill.   II. Title
PZ8.S64Pr   1995
[398.21—dc20]
[Fic]   94-32497
Manufactured in Singapore
10   9   8   7   6   5   4   3   2   1
First Edition

Source Note

I first came across a version of this story in "The Sleeping Prince," in Alison Lurie's *Clever Gretchen and Other Forgotten Folktales* (Crowell, 1980). This led me to two previous sources—"Incarnat, blanc et or" ("Rosy Red, White and Gold") by Paul Delarue (Quatre Jeudia, Paris, 1955) and an even earlier source from which it was derived, "El rey durmiente en su lecho" ("The King Sleeping in His Bed"), published in *Folklore Españolas* (Francisco Alvarez Y. C., Seville, 1886).

Two native speakers of Spanish, Diana Bartley and Elba Marrero, whose language skills make my work stronger, helped with the translation. Working from copies of the intermediate French edition and the original Spanish source, I was able to explore the possibilities in each as I developed my own retelling. My thanks to Ms. Bartley and Ms. Marrero.

—J. W. S.

Once upon a time, there lived a king and queen who dearly loved their only daughter. Her name was Florecita, which means "little flower." One midwinter day, as Princess Florecita sat at her window sewing with a golden thimble, she pricked her finger, and a drop of blood fell on the sill. At that moment, a little black bird in the tree outside began to sing:

> *"Over the hills, through woods so deep,*
> *A gentle prince lies asleep, asleep."*

The princess was struck by these words and called out, "Pray, little chango, sing again."
And the bird sang:

"Under a wicked spell he'll stay,
His life slipping away, away."

The princess cried, "Pray, little chango, sing again." And the bird sang:

"Only a maid can set things right,
He wakes but once, on Midsummer Night."

"Tell me, what does your song mean?" asked the princess gently.

So the bird began to speak. "In a distant castle there dwells the noblest and most
handsome prince in the world, with skin as white as snow, lips as red as blood, and hair as
golden as the sun. People the world over marvel at his kind heart, his generous nature, and
his good will."

"Why does he sleep?" asked Florecita.

The bird hopped onto Florecita's hand. "A wicked magician, envying the prince, has bewitched him. He wakes but once a year, on Midsummer Eve, then falls directly to sleep again. Thus it will be until the end of time."

"Can nothing be done to help him?"

"Nothing, unless a maiden, watching beside his bed, were to stroke his forehead with a black feather so he might see her when he woke."

"Where does he rest?" asked the princess.

"I do not know," said the bird, "except that his castle lies far, farther, and farthest still, so that to get there you must wear out a pair of iron shoes."

With that, the little chango flipped his tail and flew away. As he did so, a black feather fluttered to the ground. The princess picked it up and put it in her pocket for safekeeping, for it seemed to her a sign.

Days passed, and try as she might, the princess could not forget the bird's song. It reminded her of a young prince who had helped her years ago. She'd been riding a new pony and had almost been thrown, but the passing stranger had gentled it. As she looked into his eyes, Florecita had seen great kindness.

At last the princess could bear these thoughts no longer and decided she must find the sleeping prince. She had a pair of iron shoes made, with sturdy hobnail soles and high tops to lace tight with woven wire. When they were ready, late one night, she put them on.

Oh, the shoes were heavy! She could barely lift one foot after another. And how they bit into her feet! But she knew it had to be thus.

Trying to ease her parents' worry, Florecita left a note on her bed table. But when the king and queen found it the next morning, they sent servants to search far and wide. Alas, the servants returned alone. The king and queen grieved terribly, for they believed their daughter was dead.

Meanwhile, the princess had set off in her iron shoes. Traveling far, farther, and farthest still, she came to a great forest. Yet she did not hesitate or turn aside, but stroked her feather for courage and trudged straight into its terrible darkness.

Late one evening she came upon a lonely cottage, tucked snugly between two trees in a clearing. When she knocked at the door, an old woman, an *anciana*, opened it, and asked what she wanted.

"I am searching for the castle of the sleeping prince," said Florecita bravely. "Do you know where it is?"

"Not I, but I can give you a bite to eat and a drop to drink," said the old woman, taking pity on Florecita. "Then you'd best go back from where you came, for this is no place for any mortal."

"No," said the princess. "I must go on."

"If you must, you must," said the old woman. "Come in, then, my dear, and when my son the West Wind gets home, I will ask him the way. But take care he does not see or hear you, for his temper is ferocious."

So she gave the princess some supper and hid her in a corner cupboard. Soon there was a rustling of leaves outside and in swept the West Wind. The princess peeked around the door.

"Mother," blustered the wind, "I smell mortal flesh."

"Oh, my son, it was only a poor girl in iron shoes who came by today, asking the way to the castle of the sleeping prince."

"That I do not know," said the West Wind. "She should have asked my cousin the East Wind. He may have seen it."

The next morning, when the West Wind left to blow spring rains across the countryside, the princess stumbled out of the cupboard. Seeing how the iron shoes bit into the girl's ankles, the anciana said, "Here, my dear, take this balm of lady's bedstraw to rub on your tired feet."

The princess thanked the old woman and started on her journey again. She walked far, farther, and farthest still, until at last she reached the forest's edge. Ahead she could see that the land turned marshy, yet she knew that was the way she must go. The sun scorched her and the rain soaked her, but at least the balm numbed the pain of the iron shoes.

Late one evening she came to another cottage, perched securely on posts above the water, where an anciana asked what she wanted.

"I am searching for the castle of the sleeping prince," said the princess. "Do you know where it is?"

"Not I," said the old woman, who was as pale as silver water. "But I can give you a bite to eat and a drop to drink. Then you'd best go back from where you came, for this is no place for any mortal."

"No," said the princess. "I must go on."

"If you must, you must," said the old woman. "Come in, then, my dear, and when my son the East Wind gets home, I will ask him the way. But take care he does not see or hear you."

So she gave the princess some supper and hid her in the narrow safety of the clock case.

Soon there was a lashing of rain and in rushed the East Wind, knocking over a table in his haste. Florecita could peek out from behind the pendulum and see him whirling about the room.

"Mother," shrieked the wind, "I smell mortal flesh." Florecita shivered, fearing she might be discovered. But the old woman quieted her son and then repeated Florecita's question.

"I do not know the way to the sleeping prince's castle," said the East Wind. "She should have asked my cousin the North Wind. He may have seen it."

As soon as it was light, the East Wind swept out of the house, to blow cooling breezes across the summer fields. Gingerly, Florecita climbed out of the clock case. Seeing the princess's threadbare clothes, the anciana took pity. "Here, my dear, take this shawl," she offered. "It may keep out some of the North Wind's chill breath."

The princess thanked the old woman and started on her journey again. Ahead she could see low hills turning into steeper mountains. That was the way she must go. She walked far, farther, and farthest still in her iron shoes. Despite the anciana's balm of lady's bedstraw, her feet ached with pain. Despite the shawl, the sun scorched her and the rain soaked her. Whenever she was downhearted, she stroked the little black feather. Then she felt better.

At last, late one evening, she came to another cottage, wedged in a crevasse in the mountains. The princess convinced the kindly anciana, who was as sharp and bony as a mountain peak, to let her in. After giving Florecita some supper, she hid the girl in the pantry, for she knew her son the North Wind would be returning. Soon there was a terrible blowing of snow outside and in crashed the North Wind.

As before, Florecita's question was asked, and her fear turned to delight when she heard the wind whistle in reply, "The path outside our door leads directly down the mountain to the sleeping prince's castle. But, little good it would have done your poor visitor, for the gate is guarded by two huge gryphons, who devour anyone who tries to pass."

"Is there no way for her to enter, then?" asked the anciana.

"I do not know," said the wind, "but it is said that the touch of human kindness can tame them."

As soon as it was light the next day, the North Wind stormed out, to begin bringing the chill of autumn down from the mountains. Florecita climbed out of the pantry. "Here, my dear," said the helpful anciana, "take these two white gardenias growing beside our door. They may give you courage to confront the gryphons at the castle gate."

Princess Florecita thanked the old woman and set out. She walked on far, farther, and farthest still. The sun scorched her, the rain soaked her, and the snow chilled her. When she had descended from the mountains, she looked down and saw that her iron shoes were worn completely through. Joyfully she threw them off.

She looked up, and ahead were the castle's golden towers, with two gryphons guarding the gate. When they caught sight of Florecita, they growled fiercely and pawed the ground with curled talons.

Though the princess wanted to run away, she ventured closer. "I've come much too far," Florecita thought to herself, "to turn back now." Just as the gryphons drew back to spring at her, she offered up the gardenias. At once the gryphons were as tame as kittens. The princess stroked them gently, then strode into the castle.

Inside she found many rooms, each more magnificently furnished than the one before. But everyone was in a deep sleep. In the kitchen, cooks slept in front of their stoves. The palace cat slept next to a hen waiting to become Sunday dinner. In the pantries, butlers slept beside the silver they'd been polishing. And in the halls, maids slept beside their brooms. Try as she might, Florecita could not wake them.

At last the princess came to a bedchamber hung with curtains of silver, held back with clasps of gold. Before her lay the sleeping prince, who seemed to her the handsomest man in the world. His skin was as white as snow, his lips as red as blood, and his hair as golden as the sun.

The princess sat down beside his ebony bed and waited. She had walked for many weeks, and it was now Midsummer Eve. At midnight the tower clock began to strike, and slowly the prince started to stir.

Remembering the little chango's words, the princess drew the feather across his forehead. Again and again she stroked his brow until at last the prince opened his eyes.

Seeing the poor maid beside him, he reached for her hand. "Who are you, my dear?" he asked.

Before the princess could answer, there arose a huge clamor. Horses began to neigh and chickens to cluck. Cooks rattled pans, gardeners clattered watering cans, and stableboys shook harnesses. But the prince paid no heed to any of this, for he was smitten by the princess. "Whoever you are, my life belongs to you," he said softly, as he looked into her eyes with the same kindness she remembered from long ago. "Will you marry me?"

When the princess returned his gaze, she saw that he was as good and brave as he was handsome. "My name is Florecita, and my journey has been long to rescue you." After telling her tale, she said, "I will marry you, with all my heart."

So the prince and princess rode to the castle of the king and queen, who were overjoyed to have their beloved daughter back. There they were wed amid great festivity. All the people in the prince's kingdom came, as did people from kingdoms far and wide. Some marveled at the princess's beauty. Others praised her determination. Still others admired her selflessness.

The prince, though he was surprised to
discover Florecita was really a princess,
could not have been happier, for he already
loved her more than all the world.